The Mercantile Owner's Bride

Mail Order Brides of Dayton Falls

(Book Three)

Copyright

Copyright ©2019 Cheryl Wright

Dedication

To Margaret Tanner, my very dear friend and fellow author, for her enduring encouragement and friendship.

To Alan, my husband of over forty-eight years, who has been a relentless supporter of my writing and dreams for many years.

To You, my wonderful readers, who encourage me to continue writing these stories. It is such a joy knowing so many of you enjoy reading my stories as much as I love writing them for you.

Table of Contents

Chapter One

Westlake, Wyoming – 1880

Phoebe Jackson stared at her reflection in the mirror.

Her face was caked in make up. She wore heavy make up, and her cheeks were powered with rouge. Her lips a dark red.

Her hair had been carefully styled to match that of all the other young women in the burlesque show.

Phoebe fingered the skimpy outfit she was wearing. With the distance they were from the stage, the audience couldn't see how worn and ragged the costumes were. They couldn't see the missing sequins, or the tiny tears.

The chunky shoes weren't much better, with their jagged edges and frayed ribbon.

But Phoebe didn't care.

She held her hands to her heart as it beat wildly. This would be her first professional performance – she'd worked long and hard to get to this point.

Her dear parents would be so proud of her. They would have attended the performance, indulged her ego, shared in her joy.

Instead, it was just her. She would pretend they were here, in the audience. She was certain they'd be smiling down on her, so proud of all she'd achieved in her short life despite all the adversity she'd faced.

At just twenty, she'd been chosen to perform – out of the 85 girls who auditioned, she was one of the chosen few. Only twelve girls made the final cut.

Her heart skipped a beat.

"It's show time!" A teenage boy shouted at them through the door. Since all the girls were in various stages of undress, he was forbidden to enter the dressing room, but they all knew he peeked when he thought he could get away with it.

Screams of delight riddled the air. Excitement practically bounced off the walls.

It was time to prove she deserved the place she'd been granted in this most prestigious of burlesque shows.

* * *

"Come on girls, keep moving." Mrs Mac, the choreographer, clapped her hands and scowled as they all ran toward the stage.

"Opening night." She took a deep breath. "It *must* be perfect – all the critics will be here. They will make or break us."

Phoebe chewed at her bottom lip. She didn't want to be the cause of their demise.

"Smile Phoebe," Mrs Mac said as the girl got closer. "You will be brilliant." She leaned closer and whispered in Phoebe's ear so the others couldn't hear. "You are one of our best dancers. You have nothing to worry about."

Phoebe's eyes sparkled, and a big smile lit up her face.

As they took their places on the stage, her heart beat rapidly, and she felt faint. *You'll be alright*, she told herself over and over.

Some of the girls stood still in their places offstage while others stretched and warmed up.

They all watched the stage manager at the side of the stage, as he counted down on his fingers. One. Two. Three.

Phoebe took a calming breath as the curtain rose for the first time.

* * *

The crowd applauded as the troupe took their final bow. It felt surreal to Phoebe; did she really dance an entire routine without stumbling?

She looked down into the audience. They were smiling, and many stood. A standing ovation; she never would have believed it.

Reporters stood to the side, scribbling down notes. What would they say? Would the critics be good to them, or would it be the end?

Her every step was perfect, she was certain. She'd soon know; she'd be hauled out back if she'd messed up. She was dreading the next few minutes.

As she glanced to her left, the stage manager stared at her, then nodded his head, a huge smile on his face. She let out the breath she didn't realize she'd been holding.

Once they finished bowing to the audience, the dancers all linked arms and danced their way back off the stage.

The applause continued and they danced back onto the stage the way they'd practiced. Once the applause began to subside, they danced off again.

Phoebe breathed a huge sigh of relief as they all dispersed.

Mrs Mac pulled her aside as they made her way back to the shared dressing room. "Perfect," she said as she clapped her hands together. "That was amazing!"

Phoebe stared into her eyes and noticed the unshed tears but didn't dare mention it.

The older woman swiped at her eyes. "You see how good you are, little one? You made me cry." She gave a little sniff. "No other dancer has ever made me cry before."

She put her arm around Phoebe's shoulder. "I have big plans for you, my dear. If you continue to work hard," She suddenly stopped and slapped her hands to her mouth.

Curious, Phoebe stepped forward and spoke. "If I continue to work hard?"

She wanted to know. She hadn't thought beyond the Burlesque Show.

Mrs Mac lowered her hands and shook her head. "I shouldn't have said anything," she said. "I don't want to give you false hope."

"*Please*," Phoebe begged. "Please tell me."

Mrs Mac took a deep breath. "You mustn't tell anyone," she whispered. "Perhaps one day, if you work hard that is…"

Phoebe waited with bated breath, desperate to know what might be in store for her.

At that moment, the manager, Mr Grayson, came along and Mrs Mac gave her a little shove. "Off you go Phoebe. Take off your make-up and get ready for bed. That's a good girl."

Phoebe tossed and turned that night, wondering what they had in store for her.

* * *

The dancers worked hard.

They practiced at least two hours a day, until Mrs Mac was happy. Then they danced at night. They did three sessions a night and were all exhausted by the time the curtain came down for the final time.

"You're doing fabulously," Mrs Mac told her one night a few months later. "As I predicted, you are our best dancer. You listen to instructions and do whatever I ask. Mr Grayson was very pleased when I told him."

Phoebe grinned.

She got little in way of payment, but all the girls got room and board for free. Plus there was a cook who looked after them.

They really wanted for nothing.

Mrs Mac stepped into her and held her shoulders.

The beloved choreographer licked her lips before continuing. "Do you know what this means, Phoebe?"

She shook her head. She really had no idea.

"Maybe, just maybe, you will get to dance in the Gentleman's Club."

Her eyes sparkled, and she had a huge smile on her face.

Phoebe did a little dance. "Really?" She almost sang the words, she was so excited.

The Gentleman's Club was in the better part of town. The façade was far more prestigious than the regular Burlesque Show where Phoebe danced, and people went there in droves.

At least that's what she'd been told.

As the name suggested, it was for gentlemen only. They paid a much higher price for entry and were treated like royalty.

So Mrs Mac said, anyway.

She couldn't stop grinning. In fact, her face hurt from smiling so much. She clasped her hands together in front of her chest as her heart beat so fast she began to feel faint. "Oh, Mrs Mac! Really?" she asked. "Are you serious? I mean…"

She didn't get to finish as the older woman intervened. "Shhhh. Remember what I said. You mustn't tell a soul."

"Enough now," Mrs Mac said. "Run along and get changed. We'll talk again another time." She put her fingers to her lips reinforcing that not a word was to be said.

Phoebe nodded, then practically skipped toward the dressing room. Her life just took a turn for the better.

Mama and Papa would have been so proud of her.

Chapter Two

Outside of performance times, there was little to keep the girls occupied.

They had two hours of rehearsals a day, and two hours of performing. Because they weren't allowed to go out unaccompanied, for their own safety of course, they usually sat around talking. Besides they were generally too tired to do much else.

The other girls in the troupe were in the same position as Phoebe. Their parents were also deceased.

As an only child, she was an orphan, alone in the world. She often felt totally alone despite being surrounded by eleven other young women.

"Shall we venture into town?" What she wouldn't give do to browse the dressmaker's shop and see the wonderful array of gowns they had on display there?

"That would be wonderful!" All the young ladies were quite excited at the prospect, but Phoebe was aware it could never come to fruition.

They would never be given permission without a chaperone, and that would take all the fun out of going.

She sat back in her seat and thought about all the possibilities – if she hadn't joined the Burlesque Show.

After all, she had a contract, and if she didn't fulfil it, she would have to pay a fortune to secure her release. Mrs Mac had told her this time and again. It was a legal document and there were severe penalties, even jail, if she broke the contract.

* * *

Several of the women in Dayton Falls had suggested it, noticing how overwhelmed he'd become at the Mercantile on a daily basis. And now Edward Horvard decided it was time. He needed a wife.

The problem was, Dayton Falls had a distinct shortage of eligible unmarried women. Both the sheriff and the barber had acquired their wives via a mail order bride agency in Westlake Wyoming, but Edward did not want to stoop to that level.

With the small influx of mail order brides, the town had grown. Not only with women, but also the babies they were producing.

In turn, they needed more supplies. He was struggling to keep up.

There were supplies to order, stocktakes to undertake, not to mention storing and shelving all the supplies and serving in the store.

He'd always prided himself on being independent, and not needing any help. But lately it had become way too much for him to handle.

He'd always believed if the Good Lord wanted him to have a wife, he would have brought a suitable wife to him. But it had become abundantly clear that was not about to happen.

If he wanted a wife, he'd have to make it happen.

* * *

Every day the girls rehearsed. At least two hours a day. It was tiring.

"The routine *must* be perfect," Mrs Mac would tell them. Anyone who messed up was slapped across the legs with a cane stored slightly off-stage for that very reason.

Phoebe was determined never to feel the sting of that cane or endure the wrath of Mrs Mac.

There was no favoritism, so despite what Mrs Mac had said to her, Phoebe always did her best.

She'd managed to stay clear of the wicked cane so far, touch wood.

Whether that was good luck or skill on the stage, she wasn't sure, but she had no intention of being on the wrong end of the punishment that had been dished out to more than half the troupe so far.

As they entered the dressing room after their performance, that night, Phoebe noticed the other girls whispering. Everyone knew the secret apparently, except her.

"What's going on?" She hadn't made any close friends since arriving, so wasn't sure she'd find out.

"There's a rumor going around," Gemma whispered. "Apparently they're moving you to the Gentleman's Club. Very soon."

Phoebe squealed with delight.

"Shhh," the dancer told her. "No one is supposed to know. Especially you."

Phoebe slapped her hands to her mouth.

"It won't be much different," she continued. "More money though, or so I've heard."

Not that having money of her own had done much good. The girls in the troupe were virtual prisoners. To protect their reputations, they were told.

Her hands were sweaty. She could barely contain her excitement as she endeavored to remove her make up; she wondered if it were really true. After all, she'd only been part of the show for a mere six months. Surely there were others who were far more qualified.

Clara leaned toward Phoebe and whispered so only she could hear. "It's a trap. Get out. Run."

Phoebe was confused. "Get out? What do you mean…?"

"The Gentleman's Club is a place where men, uh," Her eyes looked about the room. Everywhere except at Phoebe.

She watched expectantly. "Where men what?" she asked innocently.

"I'll just come out and say it," Clara said. "Where men pay for women's services." She stared directly into Phoebe's face. "You'll become a prostitute if you go there. Better to run."

Suddenly the door opened and Mr Grayson, the troupe manager, stormed in without care for the state of undress the dancers were in.

"Phoebe!" he shouted across the room.

She sat planted to her seat, terror shuddering through her body. He stomped up to where she sat and wrenched her by the arm. "Grab your things from your room, Phoebe." "You're leaving for the Gentlemen's Club. I'll wait outside."

She was in shock and couldn't move.

* * *

Clara leaned forward and hugged Phoebe tightly. "Get out," she said quietly. "Climb out the window and run. Don't look back."

"I'll miss you," Clara said loudly. "Take care." She pulled the still shocked Phoebe to her feet and pushed her in the direction of Mr Grayson.

"Hurry up," the older man shouted. "I don't have all day."

Phoebe ran past him toward her room. "I won't be long, Mr Grayson," she said, trying to hide her terror. "I'll just grab my things."

He mumbled under his breath, and Phoebe thought it sounded like "Not that you'll need clothes." When she looked back, he had a leering smirk on his face.

Her heart thudded. Clara must be right. They were going to use her like a piece of meat to satisfy the needs of upper-class gentlemen.

She'd been told more than once she was pretty, even beautiful. That's probably all that was needed to qualify. That and being female.

Her heart began to pound. She continued to run. The quicker she got to her room, the more time she had to leave. If she didn't get away before Mr Grayson arrived...

She didn't want to think about it.

She ran to her room and locked the door. She didn't have a lot of possessions and grabbed the meagre items she did own, shoving them into her tattered carpetbag.

As quietly as she could manage, she slid open the bedroom window. Many a night she'd opened that window to let in the fresh air. With six of them sharing room, it was stuffy at night, and she could barely breath sometimes.

"Phoebe, hurry up!" Mr Grayson rattled the door as he yelled to her.

"I won't be long, Mr Grayson," she called back. "I'm just changing my clothes," she said, as she dangled one foot onto the small bush that stood back from the window. All she had to do now was manage not to fall.

If that happened, she would be doomed to the Gentlemen's Club, and there would be no saving her.

She put one foot to the top of the bush and clung to the window ledge as she balanced herself. Mr Grayson continued to rattle the door handle, but now he was also pounding on the door.

She was terrified he was going to break the door down and burst into the room at any moment. She had to be on the ground before that happened or she would be doomed.

Her carpetbag was holding her back. She couldn't climb down the bush while juggling the bag, so threw it to the ground.

She cringed at the loud thud it made as it hit the ground.

"What the hell are you doing, Phoebe?" Mr Grayson snarled. She could hear him banging against the door, trying to break it down. "Where's the damned key?" he demanded, still pounding away, trying to gain entrance.

She knew the moment he'd got inside the room. He let out a string of expletives when he discovered the room empty.

Cringing within the bush, pulling her bag in with her, within seconds of hearing Mr Grayson's voice closer than was comfortable, she began shaking and crying at the same time. She slapped a hand across her mouth, trying to stifle any sound she might make.

"Damn girl is gone," he shouted, storming out of the room above her.

Phoebe stayed where she was until she thought it was safe to leave. She couldn't risk being seen in the daylight.

It was pitch black by the time she left her hiding place.

But what would she do now?

She'd grown up not far from Westlake but had never been out alone in the darkness. Or the daylight for that matter.

After all the lights had gone out in the building, she crept quickly away from the Burlesque Theatre. A place she wished she'd never set eyes on.

Phoebe wandered the streets in the dark, until she came to a small laneway.

The main road was terrifying to her – men looked her up and down, as she still wore her flimsy dance outfit.

One seedy looking character lurched toward her. She screamed then ran in the opposite direction, until she came across the place she now stood.

It was not well lit, but the one lantern gave out enough light that she could see almost to the end. She didn't know what was down that laneway but had no choice but to take the chance. At least she would be off the main streets and out of sight should Mr Grayson decide to come searching for her.

Clutching tightly to her carpetbag, she made her way further down the street until she came across a two-storey building.

There was a brass plate on the pillar, but she couldn't make it out in the dark. A narrow stairway led to a room at the top.

She gingerly climbed the steps, anxious there might be someone up there who might attack her. She was completely alone, and very vulnerable.

Once up there, she could see all the way to both ends of the street. She would see someone approaching and would most certainly see Mr Grayson.

She crouched down in the corner of the little balcony she found at the top of the rickety steps.

Clutching her carpetbag, she slid to the ground, and squatted. What she would do next, she had no idea.

She forced her eyes to stay open – she could not defend herself if she fell asleep.

* * *

Phoebe lay huddled in the corner of the small balcony. She sensed someone was there before she'd even opened her eyes.

She slowly opened them keeping her head low, hoping to have an advantage over them when she ran for her life.

It was daylight, but she had no idea what time it was.

She smelled the light perfume and noticed the long skirt before even lifting her head. As she slowly scanned higher, she saw the woman was well dressed, her hair pulled back in a tidy bun.

"And who might you be?" The voice was soft but authoritive.

She reached down, her hand wavering in mid-air. Reluctantly, Phoebe lifted her hand. Not only was it freezing cold, it was shaking. A testament of the terror she'd faced the previous night.

After all, who was to say this woman hadn't been sent by Mr Grayson?

"You first," she said, suspicion obvious in her voice.

The woman nodded. "Alright, that's fair. I am Miss Bethany Wilde. I own this agency."

Phoebe's head shot up. "Agency? What agency?"

Miss Bethany Wilde let out a sigh. "I own the Mail Order Bride Agency," she said. "This is my office." She pointed toward the locked door, then pulled a key out of her reticule and placed it in the lock.

"You're shivering my dear, and no wonder! Look at that skimpy outfit you're wearing."

Thank goodness for the flimsy jacket she had shoved into her carpetbag. She'd be frozen to death if not for that.

Miss Bethany waved Phoebe into the sparse room. There was little more than a desk with a chair either side, and some files sitting on the ornately carved desk.

"Sit down, my dear," she said, busying herself with the woodfire in the corner. "What did you say your name was?"

Phoebe knew full well she hadn't disclosed her name to this total stranger. According to Mrs Mac,

Mr Grayson had invested a lot in training her, so she would put nothing past him to get her back.

She glared at the other woman and sat silently.

Once the fire was lit, warmth soon engulfed the room. Miss Bethany took her place behind the desk, and Phoebe moved closer to the fire, still clutching tightly to her bag. All her worldly goods were in that bag. Not that they amounted to much.

She extended her hands toward the heat and could feel the other woman's eyes burn a hole in her back.

"My dear girl, I am not going to harm you."

Phoebe looked back over her shoulder. She seemed harmless enough but continued to stare.

"You've obviously endured a severe trauma. And your clothing," she waved towards the skimpy outfit Phoebe wore. "Where have you come from, the dance hall?"

"The Burlesque Show," she blurted out before she realized what she was saying. She stared for a moment before continuing. Miss Bethany looked appropriately shocked, so perhaps it was safe after all. "I, I had to escape, before it was too late," she said quietly.

"Escape? My dear girl, what on earth happened?"

Phoebe retold the entire story, right down to the fact she was to be shipped off to the Gentleman's Club under false pretenses.

Miss Bethany sat there solemnly, her eyes wide with shock.

"Tell me, Phoebe," she said, finally prizing her name out of the intrude., "What are you going to do now?" She fiddled about with the files on her desk, putting a small pile of handwritten letters in front of her.

Phoebe straightened her shoulders and sat straighter in the chair. "I have no idea. I've got no money, and don't know what to do." Tears began to roll down her face. Until now, she hadn't thought about the future. But she knew one thing, she had to leave Westlake as quickly as possible.

"I have an idea." Miss Bethany pushed several of the handwritten letters in front of her. "These gentlemen are all looking for a mail order bride. I have six letters here, all from young men looking for a wife."

"A wife?" Phoebe blurted out. "I don't want to get married!"

The shock on the other woman's face was almost comical. "What? Never?" She continued to push the letters toward Phoebe. "I have vetted these letters, and they all seem quite genuine and sound like lovely gents."

Phoebe nodded and took the proffered letters. Understanding finally dawned. It would be a way to get out of town and away from Mr Grayson's clutches.

She had no family here, and no reason to stay. She looked down at the letters in her hands. The first one was from a butcher from a small town just a few hours away. That might not be as safe as it seemed. Further away would be better.

The next one was a little further west, but perhaps still not far enough.

She continued reading until she read the Mercantile owner's letter. He lived in a small town in another state. Dayton Falls Montana. She'd never heard of it, which meant perhaps Mr Grayson also hadn't heard of it.

She pictured high class ladies visiting the Mercantile for all their necessities.

It could be fun. And she would be far away from the Burlesque. As far away as she could imagine getting.

Did she want to get married? Because that would be part of the deal.

"What does he look like, this Mercantile owner?"

Miss Bethany smiled. "He does sound nice, but he didn't send a photograph. Most of them don't." She shuffled through her files again. "But he did send a railway ticket and some money to assist his bride to get to him."

Phoebe's eyes lit up. That would certainly solve her problem of no money.

"I do hope you have another outfit. You can't travel on the railway looking like *that*." Her disgust at the skimpy outfit, as she had called it earlier, was obvious.

Opening her carpetbag, she pulled out the only other piece of clothing she had. "I have this. It's a bit tattered, but it's all I have."

"Then it will have to do."

Chapter Three

Edward Horvard stood stiffly behind the counter and glanced around.

There was only one customer left in the store. "I have to close shortly," he said. "For about an hour. If you could bring your purchases up to the counter?"

"But I'm not finished yet," Mrs Green said indignantly. She waved her long shopping list in the air.

He walked over to her. "I'll finish up for you, *and* I'll deliver it later," he said quietly. "No charge."

She stared at him.

"Just this once. I have to collect someone from the train station." He pulled his apron up over his head and rolled his sleeves down, then began to put on his jacket which had been placed on the back of a chair. He carefully hung that jacket up each morning, but rarely wore it. Only if it was extra cold.

Or something special was happening. Like today. Something markedly special was about to happen.

His new bride was arriving shortly.

He hadn't expected her so soon. In fact, he hadn't expected to hear anything back for quite some time, but the telegram announced her arrival.

He checked his pocket-watch, then hurried Mrs Green out the door. "I do apologize, Mrs Green," he said. "But I cannot be late to the station."

She nodded but he was aware she reluctantly left the store.

He turned over the sign on the door, indicating he would be back in one hour. Just enough time to pick up his new bride and take her to the church to get married.

Edward rubbed his hands together. Despite being disinclined to begin with, perhaps even now, he had been looking forward to this day since he wrote to the Mail Order Bride Agency.

Today was to be the beginning of his new life.

He wondered what his bride would look like.

"Good morning, Edward." Charlie Jones stood outside his barber's shop, waiting for customers to arrive.

"Good morning, Charlie." He pulled on his scarf and gloves as he rushed toward the train station. Any other day he would stay and chat. But not today.

He couldn't be late picking up his bride. What would she think of him if he left her standing there alone?

It was a bit of a walk, but he didn't think she would mind. He usually took the wagon to the train station, but generally when he went, he was collecting supplies.

Not today. Today was different.

He held the rumpled telegram in his hand.

11.15 – his bride would arrive in five minutes. He'd better hurry; he didn't want to be late.

The train pulled in as he arrived on the platform.

The Station Master held his flag out to keep visitors at bay. "Stand back everyone. I don't want any injuries today."

A mother grabbed her toddler as it ventured too close to the train. Edward smiled, amused at the stern look on the Station Master's face. "Madam," he said. "Please control that child."

Once the train came to a complete standstill, Edward moved closer. He had no idea how he would recognize his bride. He had no photograph of her, nor she of him.

It could be a farcical escapade for sure.

People poured out of the carriages, mostly women accompanied by their husbands. In some cases, there were young children too. He could discount those women.

He stood waiting for more than fifteen minutes and was certain she'd missed the train. It was a long trip from Wyoming, a very long trip. Perhaps she'd alighted at the incorrect station.

He certainly hoped not. It would be almost impossible to find her if that were the case.

Finally, a young woman alighted the train. She looked disheveled and disoriented and was clutching a carpetbag that had seen better days.

He moved toward her cautiously. "Miss Jackson?" he asked quietly. When she nodded slightly, he continued. "I am Edward Horvard. Your betrothed."

She looked him up and down, her mouth hanging slightly open. He felt disappointment – she wasn't expecting someone like him. That was apparent.

Her flaming red hair had been tied up in a chignon at some point but was now falling out at several places. It was all he could do not to reach out and push it back and make her more presentable.

Edward felt sorry for her. She'd spend over a week on the train. He'd sent her a ticket for her travel, and some money to ensure she was well fed on the trip, but she looked all skin and bone.

The dress she wore had seen better days. He had no idea such a trip would be detrimental to her health or her appearance.

"Miss Jackson?" he asked again, since she still hadn't acknowledged verbally whether she was indeed his intended.

She suddenly reached up and brushed her hair behind her ears. "Dearie me," she said in a rush. "I must look a fright." With a slight of hand, she released her long flowing hair from its restraints and ran her fingers through it.

Just as quickly, she had it pulled back into a semblance of order.

He stood back and stared. With her hair off her face, he could see her better. Really see her. She was a pretty little thing. In fact, he was certain she was beautiful under all that soot.

He put his hand to the small of her back and faced her in the right direction. "Let's go home," he said. "You can have a warm bath and start to feel presentable."

* * *

Phoebe slid down into the inviting bath. It was a very long time since she'd had the luxury of a bath. The dancers were not allowed that indulgence, and soon after her parents had died, she'd been shipped off to the orphanage.

They certainly didn't allow them there. A lick and a promise with a bowl of water was the closest they got to a bath.

She closed her eyes and slid lower. The warm water was like music to her aching body. Riding the railway was not the fun thing it was made out to be. Especially after so many agonizing days.

She savored the heat and the bubbles and appreciated the effort it had taken for her soon-to-be-husband to organize it for her.

She washed her hair and rinsed it carefully. She hated to think how much of that horrible soot had been caught up in her locks.

As he walked her to the bathroom, she had spotted the bedroom. *His bedroom* – she hoped there was another room for her.

They were complete strangers, so she hoped he didn't expect…

She shook herself mentally.

Mr Horvard seemed nice enough, and he'd been a perfect gentleman. He'd given her some towels and told her to take her time.

When she'd first arrived, he'd taken her into the store and told her to choose a pretty dress and some undergarments. Did he know she was destitute? She was appalled at the situation she now found herself in.

But then again, perhaps he wanted to ensure his soon-to-be-bride looked presentable. A male pride kind of thing.

She put her hands to her heart when she realized it would only be a matter of hours. perhaps less, and she would no longer be Miss Phoebe Jackson.

Instead she would be Mrs Edward Horvard.

She hadn't expected it to be so quickly, but Mr Horvard, Edward, told her they were to be married later that day.

The more she thought about it, the better it seemed. She couldn't afford to tarnish her reputation by staying with an unmarried man, alone in his house – she would be branded a hussy.

And she was far from that. It was the exact reason she'd fled the Burlesque.

She heard a tap on the door. "Miss Jackson? Phoebe?" he called through the door. "As soon as you're ready, we'll head to the church."

His footsteps on the wooden floorboards alerted her that he'd already returned to the store where he said he would be waiting.

She knew he was the Mercantile owner, that much was in his letter, but she hadn't expected the store to be so big. Nor did she expect to see the wide array of items that he carried.

His letter hadn't said much. *Hardworking, Christian storeowner seeks wife. Required to tend to house and help in store occasionally.*

That was the full extent of his introduction.

To be fair, he didn't have time to get to know her, nor she him. But he seemed nice enough.

She was here now, and about to be wedded. She would find out soon enough exactly what was expected of her. She'd come so far to marry this stranger, and she wasn't about to turn back now.

Besides, where would she go? She had broken her contract and was now a wanted woman.

Chapter Four

It was a short walk to the Dayton Falls church.

"Up the road and around the corner," Edward had said, and that's exactly where it was.

She could feel strange eyes on her as he walked her down the main street before they turned the corner to the church. She was certain the town's people were wondering who this strange woman was, hanging off the Mercantile owner's arm.

She straightened her shoulders and clung to him a little tighter.

When they arrived at the small church, Edward introduced her to the preacher. He looked her up and down, and for a preacher, he didn't seem too friendly toward her.

He went to the back of the church to prepare, and Edward explained he was not very amenable toward mail order bride marriages.

Phoebe glanced down at her dress. It was pretty, but was it pretty enough to be a wedding dress? She had always dreamed of being a beautiful bride dressed all in white, with a long train trailing behind her.

As though he could read her thoughts, Edward leaned close to her and whispered. "You look beautiful." He reached over and brushed her hair back behind her ears. When she was dancing, her hair was always up, and he wouldn't have been able to do that.

Smiling, she nodded, then stared at the preacher as he prepared for their marriage.

At that moment she vowed to be a good wife. To prove to the preacher that all things were possible, that because love wasn't involved, it didn't mean they couldn't make a good marriage.

Because she was certain they could; would make sure they did.

The preacher nodded. Edward looked down at her again and smiled. He squeezed her hand, then led her toward the altar, where they would say their vows.

With his bible held open in his hands, the preacher began the ceremony.

It seemed like forever later when he finished. "I now pronounce you man and wife. May love abound." He stared at them both. Phoebe was certain it was a message for them both. To affirm that mail order marriages wouldn't last.

"You may kiss the bride," he finally told Edward, and slammed the bible closed, as though by doing so he was making a statement about his opinion of this particular marriage.

Edward turned toward her. He was beaming and looked extremely happy. He leaned in to her, his face only a breath away from hers.

Her heart began to beat rapidly at the prospect.

His eyes stared into hers. They were so close it almost made her giddy.

She closed her eyes and stepped back slightly, losing her balance as she did so.

His arms were around her before she could fall.

He was gentle and strong at the same time. She stared up into his face. His hair had fallen across his eyes, and she brushed it away.

"Ahem." The preacher cleared his throat in order to get their attention.

Edward straightened up, pulling her with him.

Phoebe felt herself blush. She would have melted into the ground if she could.

"Thank you, Preacher," Edward said quietly, then hooked her arm through his and led her back to the Mercantile. To his home.

Their home. The place she was meant to spend the rest of her life.

* * *

"And this is the storeroom. When new items arrive each month, items that will fit, go out on the shelves. Those that don't, they go in here."

Phoebe nodded and bit her bottom lip. There was so much to remember, and she worried it would all be quickly forgotten.

"I don't expect you to remember all this," he said softly. He brushed a finger gently across her cheek, then swiftly pulled it away.

He put a hand to her back and led her to the residence. "I think that's enough for today. Go and put your things away." She stared at him blankly.

"Oh," he said. "You don't know where. I'll come too."

She stared at the floor. "Apart from this lovely dress you gave me, I only have a one dress, and a few undergarments. I won't need much space."

He frowned. She wasn't sure if he was shocked or angry. "In that case, come with me."

Now it was her turn to frown.

He led her back to the rack her wedding dress came from. "Take your pick – whatever you need." He was beaming. Was he happy to provide for his bride?

She shook her head. He shouldn't have to supply all her clothing.

"It will be my pleasure to ensure my bride is beautifully clothed," he said softly. There was no one in the store except the two of them as the "closed" sign was still on the door. She wondered if perhaps he was aware of her deep embarrassment.

She really had no choice. She only had the one tardy dress she arrived in, plus her wedding gown. She would keep that to become her Sunday best.

"Really Mr Horvard," she said equally quietly. "I can't accept your offer. It's too much."

He frowned. "Edward, please. We are husband and wife, you can't go around calling me Mr Horvard." He grinned and she felt relieved. He seemed a kindly man.

He pulled several beautiful dresses off the rack and held them in front of her. "These will do nicely, but if you don't like them, feel free to choose different ones."

She shook her head again. "No, they're beautiful. Thank you, Mr… er, Edward."

He grinned and guided her toward the undergarments. "Take whatever you need." He picked up a chemise and some drawers and fiddled with them. "I'll leave you to choose whatever you need of these. And don't forget nightgowns."

He left her alone and went behind the counter, to finish off some paperwork, he'd told her.

"I'll show you where to place your clothes, and then I must reopen the store," he said, pointing to the door. "I can see customers wanting to come in."

Despite his offer, she only took one dress, and one change of undergarments, as well as a nightgown. She'd managed on little before, and she could do it again – she wouldn't be a burden.

Holding tight to her new clothes, the first new garments she could ever recall having, she turned away. "You go and attend your customers. I'll be fine," she said, then scampered into the private residence, which was off the store.

Despite having been in there earlier for her bath, it was all new to Phoebe. She'd been so nervous before, she hadn't really taken much in.

There appeared to be three bedrooms, but two of them were taken up with storage. The master bedroom was the only room with an actual bed. She shuddered.

She'd hoped to spend her wedding night alone, but it wasn't to be.

The bathroom was huge. She knew that from her earlier encounter.

The clawfoot tub was enormous, and she'd enjoyed sliding right down into it. It had been a welcome relief after the vulgar amenities available at the Burlesque.

A bowl of cold soapy water, used by many, was not her idea of cleanliness.

She was certain Mrs Mac and Mr Grayson did not endure the same facilities.

If she didn't understand before, she did now – Edward Horvard was quite well off. One could almost say rich. His bathroom was bigger than the two bedrooms currently used for additional storage. And it had running water.

But above all, the indoor privy was the thing that really caught her attention. It seemed she would live a life of luxury if she played her cards right.

Last of all she checked the room at the back of the flat. She found a tiny kitchen there.

Tiny in her terms at least. At the orphanage the kitchen was quite large. It was similar at the Burlesque. Cook had many mouths to feed so it was understandable.

Phoebe had never cooked a meal in her life and wasn't sure where to start. She filled the kettle with water, so at least Edward could have coffee when he was ready. She would come back later to prepare his luncheon but at this stage, had no idea of what she would make.

Close to the kitchen was a small reception room. She eyed off the cozy-looking couch.

Finally, she returned to the master bedroom where she'd deposited her newly acquired clothing and changed into her other new dress, rather than risk ruining her Sunday best. It was a luxury she'd never had before.

She pulled her long hair into an acceptable style and peered at herself in the full-length mirror.

She hoped she was acceptable as the Mercantile owner's wife. She was sure he would tell her if she wasn't.

"Phoebe, my dear." She heard him call from the store via the main door to the residence. "Do you have a moment to come here?"

She was rather taken back to find a group of women staring as she entered the Mercantile.

Edward pulled her to his side. "May I introduce my beautiful wife, Phoebe?"

Beaming faces looked her over.

Women stepped forward and took her hand. "Welcome, my dear," came from many directions.

"Phoebe, I know it's too much to remember, but this is Mrs Jensen, Mrs Green, Mrs Jackson, and Mrs Grogan. They are all very happy to meet you, I'm sure."

She felt overwhelmed and clung to her husband. He slid his arm around her as though he understood.

"Now ladies, can I help anyone?"

Mrs Jensen stepped forward. Or was it Mrs Jackson? She'd eventually work them all out.

Phoebe shadowed her husband, watching and learning. One day she hoped to be an enormous help to him. To not only to keep house, but to also relieve him of some of his duties in the store.

He turned to her and nodded as though he appreciated her presence.

He pulled her closer. Phoebe was still getting used to being a married woman and wondered if they would endure.

* * *

Edward closed the store for luncheon.

It felt as though the store had been closed most of the day, but he had to eat.

He entered the residence excitedly, wondering what Phoebe had prepared. He found her exactly where he'd expected – in the well-equipped kitchen.

Nothing but the best.

He'd built this place from scratch, with the intention of one day having a wife and children. He'd come from money, and spared no expense with building this establishment, and preparing for his future.

His father had taught him that. And now it seems, it had paid off.

She had her back to him as he entered the kitchen. She turned and placed a mug of coffee on the table. "Sit down," she said. "Your luncheon is almost ready."

She worried her bottom lip before turning back away from him. It seemed to be a habit when she was nervous.

"I, I didn't know what to make," she said apologetically as she turned to face him again. "There isn't much food to work with. And I'm not much of a cook," she added quickly.

He laughed. He couldn't help himself. She was so sweet, and so innocent.

She pouted. "It's not funny," she said, still pouting and looking rather sad.

"My dear girl," he said, trying to refrain from a full belly laugh. "You have an entire store to utilize. Anything you need, just take it."

"Oh." She looked surprised at his revelation. As though it hadn't occurred to her, and he was certain at that moment, she'd never been in a kitchen, or a store, before in her life.

She placed a plate in front of him. It contained thick sliced bread and a chunk of cheese. "I'm sorry," she said, staring at him. "I'll try to do better next time."

He watched as tears welled in her eyes and jumped up from the table.

His arms were around her before he realized what he was even doing. "Don't cry," he said, lifting her chin toward him. He wiped at a stray tear that slid down her face. "You're too pretty to cry."

She leaned into him, and he heard her sniff.

It felt nice to hold her like this. To comfort her. He really had no idea what he'd been missing all these years. His life had revolved around working in the store, replenishing stocks, and filling the shelves.

At night he was exhausted, and was simply putting something together that would fill his belly. On the odd occasion, he would be invited to dine with one of the town's families.

He suddenly had a revelation. "I have some cookbooks in the store," he said. "Later, we'll look them over and find one that may help."

She wiped at her eyes and nodded. "Sounds like a good idea," she said softly.

He tightened his hold on her until she pulled out of his arms.

Edward took the hint and sat down again. The food was ordinary, but better than he might have prepared for himself.

The next few weeks could be interesting – with a new bride who had no idea how to be a wife.

* * *

Phoebe cleaned the kitchen until it was spotless, then went to find the cookbooks Edward had mentioned.

The first one she picked up was "High Class Cookery Made Easy." She stared at it, then replaced it on the shelf. She was going to struggle to make easy recipes, let alone *high class*.

"This one is meant to be good. Nearly all the ladies in town have bought it." He handed her a cookbook that wasn't too thick, but not too thin.

Cookery for the Modern Woman

She read the table of contents. It had a good variety. Lastly, she flicked through the book and read some of the recipes. They seemed fairly straightforward.

"I think that will do nicely," she said, a smile forming on her face. She was starting to relax. Edward was not demanding like she expected. In fact, was the total opposite.

She acknowledged she was totally clueless, but he was being quite the gentleman about it.

"I'll go and work something out for supper, shall I?" she asked. She didn't want to do anything that might upset him.

"Perfectly fine. Any supplies you need, come here and get it, or let me know and I'll bring it to you." She nodded and left.

"Phoebe," he called after her. "I want you to treat this store like your own personal pantry."

"Ooh, lucky lady," she heard one of the customers say. And she realized that customer was right. One day she might actually appreciate it.

Back in the kitchen, she rummaged through the drawers and finally found paper and a pencil. She would choose some recipes and check what ingredients she needed.

Once chosen, she searched the kitchen pantry. It was near empty. She found a packet of flour, but it was full of little creatures. Weevils? Disgusting.

Luckily, she had her own personal pantry downstairs. She smiled at the thought. This could be fun.

Tonight's meal would not be extravagant. She was convinced she'd never manage extravagant. Simple was definitely the way to go. Simple but hearty. That cookbook was all about hearty and uncomplicated.

Phoebe was positive it was going to be her new best friend.

When she snuck into the store a short time later, she was hoping not to distract her husband from his work. *Husband. Would she ever get used to that?*

He'd just finished serving a customer and opening the door for her, when he spotted her. "To what do I owe this pleasure," he asked, beaming at her.

"I'm in need of an apron, if you have one," she said quietly, ensuring the other customers didn't hear. "Please," she added quickly.

He grinned. "Follow me." He pointed to a corner which stored a collection of crisp white aprons. Some were quite plain, and others had a small amount of embroidery. There were also a few in pastel colors.

She reached for a plain one, but he insisted on a fancier one. She was learning it was better not to argue with him over his choices. As she turned to go back inside, he slapped her playfully on the behind.

She turned to him annoyed, and he was grinning. She was sure she had an expression of shock on her face, but he just laughed.

Now that she was his wife, he was entitled to such liberties, but they'd been married less than a day. She didn't expect that sort of behavior.

She scuttled away before he could do anything more outlandish.

Chapter Five

The cookbook proved helpful.

Once her menu was finalized, Phoebe returned to the Mercantile once again. This time with a list of items she needed to prepare supper.

She'd decided on biscuits and a hearty vegetable soup. Having all the ingredients readily available was a nice bonus she hadn't thought about.

The store was quite busy when she returned.

Edward stood behind the counter looking very important. And he was. Without the Mercantile, the town's women would have to travel quite a distance for their supplies. At least that's what Edward had told her.

"Flour, eggs, milk." She checked her list again. "Butter." She moved to the other side of the store and carefully chose the vegetables she needed. She decided not to include meat this time, since she didn't know her way around the town as yet.

He whispered in her ear. "What's for supper?"

She put a hand to her chest. "Oh my goodness, Edward. You startled me."

He stood behind her and wrapped an arm around her waist. "What's for supper," he asked more softly.

She turned around in his arms. "It's a surprise," she said cheekily. "You'll find out at supper time."

Basket in hand, she retreated to their private kitchen, but not before he sneaked a look at her *purchases*. A frown crossed his face. Good. He couldn't work out what she was cooking.

She turned back to see him rubbing his hands together. This was going to be fun.

Or it might be a disaster. She'd soon find out.

The soup was bubbling on the stove, and she was careful not to let it burn. The cookbook warned about that.

She took a spoon and tasted it. The soup was cooked, but she wasn't sure if it was good enough for her new husband. It tasted fine to her, but what sort of standards did Edward have?

She was used to the very bland and ordinary food dished out at the Burlesque by a cook who admitted she'd never had any training.

Phoebe sighed.

This was just the beginning of a long road of learning. Her biggest hope was she didn't upset Edward with her greenhorn efforts.

She stirred the soup again, then pulled the biscuits out of the oven. They looked perfect on the outside, but what about the inside?

The recipe said to rub butter over the top of the biscuits once out of the oven, so she did precisely that. She wasn't sure what it did to them, but she followed the directions to the letter.

A short time later, the table was set and ready for supper.

The kettle was almost boiling, and she had bowls ready to dish out the soup. Lastly, she went to the bathroom to freshen up, and make herself presentable.

The last thing she wanted was for Edward to think badly of her. After all, it was their first supper together and she wanted to meet his approval.

At last she heard him bid farewell to the last customer and lock the door. Then his footsteps could be heard as he entered their private domain.

It had been a long day, but she was grateful he'd taken her in. What she would have done otherwise, she had no idea.

Her life wouldn't be worth living if she'd been forced to go to the Gentlemen's Club and become a soiled dove.

Just the thought of it made her feel ill. And a little faint. She quickly sat down to recover.

"Are you alright, Phoebe?"

She hadn't heard him enter the kitchen. "I, I'm fine, thank you." She wasn't but had no intention of telling him so.

She stood, holding the back of a chair for support. "Please sit down. Supper is ready." She turned to the stove to dish up the soup. "It's not much, but it should be filling."

She placed a bowl in front of him. "Like I said earlier, I'm not a cook. I've never had to cook before, but I'm willing to learn." She smiled briefly then turned away from him to retrieve her own food.

He leaned over the soup. "It smells delicious." He took a large mouthful. "And it is delicious! This is the best meal I've had for a very long time," he said happily as he ate.

He reached across the table for a biscuit at almost the same time she did. Their hands met briefly, and she pulled hers quickly back.

He grinned at her. "I don't bite," he said, snatching up a biscuit and breaking it apart. "You've been busy," he said, shoving a piece of biscuit into his mouth.

She watched carefully to gauge his reaction. "Oh my. This is absolute bliss."

Her heart beat quickened. Did that mean her cooking met his approval? "Really?" she said softly, hardly believing her ears.

"Really," he said before taking another bite.

She leaned back in her chair. The first hurdle was over. He approved of her meal and seemed to be happy with her efforts.

"I'm not sure what you'll get tomorrow," she said apologetically, as he reached for another biscuit.

"Left over biscuits for breakfast will do just fine." He wiped at his mouth with a napkin. "If there's any of that soup left, I'll have some of that too."

He reached across the table to grab her hand. "Maybe next time you'll sit a little closer? We don't need to be opposite ends of the table."

She averted her eyes, focusing instead on their entwined hands. His were soft and warm, and very large.

He was a big man, every bit of six foot, maybe taller, while she was petit. Perfect for a dancer.

She nodded gently, and he removed his hand. It was crazy she knew, but she suddenly felt bereft. She could see herself feeling affection for this man, given time.

She mentally shook herself.

They'd been married less than a day, and already she was fantasizing about him. *What was she thinking?*

More likely than not, he had no such thoughts. She was behaving like a silly woman.

"I'll clear the table," she said when they finished, swiftly removing the dirty dishes from the table.

He was suddenly behind her – again without her realizing. The man moved so swiftly, and without noise. "Let me help," he said quietly.

She turned on him. "You'll do no such thing! You have worked hard all day." She felt offended that he would even suggest such a thing.

He put his hands out in front of him. "I didn't mean to offend or upset you," he said, hurt written all over his face. "I'm sorry," he said gently.

It was going to take time for them to get used to each other, that much was clear. She hadn't meant to hurt him, just as he hadn't meant to offend her.

"No, *I'm* sorry," she said quietly. "This is all new to me, and I'm trying to work my way through it."

He stepped forward and hugged her gently. "I understand. I'll leave you to it." He left her alone and headed toward the bedroom.

She finished cleaning the kitchen and followed him. The sleeping arrangements had been at the back of her mind for most of the day.

With only one bed, she was forced to sleep with him. Unless as she'd decided earlier, she slept on the couch.

Yes, that was a good idea – she would sleep on the couch tonight. She would have to be sneaky about it, because he probably wouldn't agree.

He was in the process of hanging up his jacket when she entered the bedroom. He had closed the curtains and turned back the bed.

The rather large bed. At both the Burlesque and the orphanage, two people slept in one small bed. The only other option was the floor. She tried that once, and it wasn't good.

She leaned in and touched the mattress. She pushed it gently – it felt soft. She hadn't slept in a soft bed for… When she thought about it, since she'd arrived at the orphanage, she'd never slept in a soft bed. Or a bed she could call her own.

She was six when her parents had died, and she vaguely remembered her mother dancing around the house. Sometimes her father would dance with her in his arms, while he danced with her mother.

It made her sad. Phoebe often thought about them, and regularly pulled out the battered photograph taken before she was born. It was the only thing she had left of them.

If only they hadn't died; she wouldn't be in this predicament if they were still around.

She shook herself. Now was not the time to become sentimental.

Edward had passed down the battered carpetbag on top of the wardrobe before he left the room.

She pulled out the battered crumpled nightgown and blanched. After seeing the new nightgown she now possessed, thanks to Edward, she couldn't imagine ever having that threadbare and yellow-stained one against her body.

The once-white nightgown was stained yellow and brown with age. It had been a hand-me-down when she first got it, and even then, it was past its prime.

She should have been disposed of it years ago, but it was the only one she had. She'd had no means to replace it despite its dilapidated state.

If she had a dollar for very time she'd ran her fingers across the almost transparent material, she would be rich. Where there was once hand embroidered flowers, there was only an outline now – the embroidery floss long gone.

She closed her eyes and recalled the joy she'd felt when she was given that worn-out nightgown. It was far better than the too tight and too old one she already had.

At least this one fit and was relatively comfortable. It might not be much, but it had been everything to her.

She was startled when he stuck his head around the door. "Don't forget your new nightgown," he said softly, staring in horror at the monstrosity she had in her hand. "We'll burn that one tomorrow."

In an instant, he was gone again. She shoved the old nightgown back into the carpetbag and placed it on a chair in the corner of the room.

She heard Edward rummaging around in the store and knew he'd return soon. She quickly changed, folding her clothes and placing them on the same chair. She heard movement close by and quickly climbed into bed.

She decided to slip out of bed once Edward was asleep and spend the night on the couch. Yes, they were married, but it didn't seem decent to sleep with a stranger, even if he was her legal husband.

She heard the bathroom door open and heart pounding, waited for Edward to return. She closed her eyes momentarily, and before long, was sound asleep.

* * *

Phoebe's eyes fluttered open and she looked around.

Panic struck her – where the heck was she?

As she slowly sat up, she noticed Edward in the bed. Now she was really panicking. She'd slept the entire night in his bed.

That hadn't been her plan, but here she was.

It was sometime around sunrise, and she gently climbed out of bed. She snatched up her clothes, and quietly went to the bathroom, being careful not to wake her husband.

More than ever, she was really beginning to appreciate that bathroom with it's extravagant privy. The likes of which she'd never seen before.

She fixed her hair using the bathroom mirror and crept out to the kitchen. There she heated the leftover soup for Edward's breakfast, and filled the kettle.

She stoked the fire the way he'd shown her and sat down at the table for a moment.

"Phoebe! Phoebe!" He called urgently.

"Edward? I'm in the kitchen."

He practically ran into the room and sat down, breathing heavily.

She stared at him. "Are you alright?" she asked, wondering what was wrong. She moved toward him and put her hand to his shoulder.

He reached up and covered her hand with his own. "I thought you'd gone," he said quietly.

She frowned. Why would he think such a thing? "I wouldn't leave you," she said softly. "You have been so kind to me."

He looked at her with relief.

The kettle began to boil, so she stepped away. He pulled her back.

"It's so nice having you here, Phoebe," he said, then gently kissed the back of her hand. The tingle that ensued frightened her momentarily.

"I, I need to attend to your breakfast." She grinned at him sitting there in his nightshirt and stepped away. She had never been treated so kindly as Edward had treated her.

He nodded and let go of her hand.

She made a mug of coffee and put it in front of him. Then she placed the biscuits in the middle of the table, along with a knob of butter.

He tucked in, obviously hungry, and she smiled. If she didn't know better, she'd think he was starving.

Last of all, she served up a big bowl of left-over soup. He lapped that up too.

She could see feeding him was going to be a big job.

"This is amazing," he said between mouthfuls.

She put her hands to her hips. "It's leftovers," she said. "Nothing special."

She made tea for herself and sat down next to him. She stared, closely watching him eat.

He watched her. "Why aren't you eating," he asked, realizing what she was doing.

She shook her head. "You first."

He dropped his food to the plate and wiped his mouth with a napkin. "You don't get to starve for my sake," he said quietly. Then his eyes opened wide. "Is that what you've done in the past?"

He was way too perceptive, and she wished he would stop.

"I don't want to talk about it," she whispered.

He reached over and broke open a biscuit, then began to butter it. He then placed it in front of her. "Please eat."

Emotion bubbled up, and she had to fight to keep her tears at bay. Was this how it would always be? With Edward looking out for her?

She was his wife, and it was her job to look after him, not the other way around. She stared into his eyes then glanced at the biscuit he was holding out to her.

"Please eat," he said again, a little more forcefully this time, but still gently.

He put the biscuit to her mouth, and she opened it slightly, taking a tiny bite. When she swallowed, he pushed the biscuit to her mouth again. This time she took a bigger bite.

He watched her every movement. Every bite she took, and every swallow that resulted. He wasn't moving until she finished, he'd told her.

When she had, he pushed her tea toward her.

Her heart pounded. Was this what marriage was like? She had no idea since she had no one to judge by.

When breakfast was finally over, Edward, who was still in his night attire, got up from the table. "I have to get ready for work now," he said. "Just know I won't have you starving yourself."

He leaned in and kissed her gently on the cheek. It still smarted even after he was gone.

Chapter Six

Edward stood behind the counter waiting for the first customers to arrive. He relished the quiet times as it meant he could check the stocks and make an order if required.

Phoebe strolled in as the first customer of the day arrived.

"You look beautiful, Phoebe," he said, but then frowned. "Isn't that the same dress you wore yesterday?" he asked quietly, out of earshot of the customer.

He watched her blush. "It is," she said equally quietly. "I can wear it for more than one day."

"Where are the others?"

She looked confused. "Others? What others?"

"Good morning Mrs Fletcher," he said jovially, turning away from his wife. Not that he felt even one bit jovial right now. He was annoyed with her. He specifically told her to take several dresses, and she obviously didn't.

"Oh, good morning, Mr Horvard," she said happily, holding a list in her hand. "Do you have time to help me out? I have quite a large list to fulfil."

He really wanted to deal with his wife's blatant defiance, but his customer had to come first. After all, without a livelihood, he wouldn't have the means to supply her with beautiful things.

"I'll just grab a box, Mrs Fletcher." He turned back to the counter but saw Phoebe out of the corner of his eye. She seemed oblivious to his annoyance.

Had he made a huge mistake marrying her? Perhaps he should have put her up at the boarding house for a few days before making the decision to wed her?

He stiffened.

It was too late now. They were married by the preacher and were legally man and wife.

Or perhaps it wasn't. *Was it too late to have their marriage annulled?*

Edward's grip on the box became so tight, a piece broke off. Trying to take his mind off Phoebe, he followed Mrs Fletcher, helping her to fill the large box he was holding.

She spotted Phoebe and near ran to reach her. "Hello, my dear," Mrs Fletcher said. "You're new in town."

Phoebe's eyes sparkled. "I'm Edward's new wife," she said cheerfully. "I'm Phoebe."

The woman stumbled backwards. "Oh my," she said, putting her hands to her chest. "You're married now, Mr Horvard? I didn't know." Then she smiled. "I am very happy for you both." She reached for Phoebe and hugged her, then just as quickly resumed her shopping.

"Do you need help," he asked his wife stiffly after Mrs Fletcher had gone. He was still annoyed with her.

But on second thought, there must be a reason for her being the way she is? That thought calmed him down, even if just for a moment or two. Until he realized that couldn't be good.

His mind went back to the tattered dress she had worn when she arrived.

The little bell over the door tinkled and Mrs Jones, the barber's wife, walked in. "Good morning," he said, a little less cheerfully, his mind still elsewhere. "Mrs Jones, please meet my wife, Phoebe."

He was proud to show her off but needed to make her understand she had a position in the community that must be upheld. And that included not wearing the same dress day after day.

The women exchanged pleasantries, then they both continued collecting up their items. Phoebe left, her arms piled with her necessities for tonight's supper. He wondered what she was making.

Edward's mind wandered for the rest of the morning, until he recalled he'd never been like this. His concentration was shot to pieces. It was not something he'd encountered before. Is that what having a wife meant? That he couldn't keep his mind on the job?

Once again, he wondered if he'd done the wrong thing in requesting a mail order bride. Especially when she'd arrived without the necessary correspondence taking place.

It really was all a mess.

His next customer arrived, and he was determined to get back to the job at hand.

And it was working, until he heard his wife singing as she went about her business. Her sweet voice travelling throughout the Mercantile.

* * *

The aromas drifting from the kitchen each day were enticing.

Phoebe may not be the best cook, but she was trying. Her efforts were certainly better than what he'd endured with his own machinations in the past. Apart from the occasional supper invitation, he near lived on beans, bread, sausages and eggs, or fried potatoes.

Edward had no idea having a wife would change his life so completely. From being deemed the most eligible bachelor in town, despite the lack of women, to suddenly having a beautiful wife.

He never thought it possible.

He had to admit though, she did seem quite naïve, and that was proving to be quite a challenge. He was used to making his own way and doing what he wanted, when he wanted. Now he was having to guide her in most things.

Edward sighed.

They'd been married a few days now, but still didn't know much about each other. Phoebe was clearly not used to hard work – every night when he came to bed, she was sound asleep.

Perhaps one day she would trust him enough to tell him what had happened to her. On second thought, he might be better off not knowing.

After the debacle of a few days ago, over her attire, he'd chosen two more dresses on her behalf and hung them in the wardrobe. She reluctantly accepted his gifts.

Over time, he hoped to understand more about her, and her needs. Her wardrobe was in need of a complete overhaul, that much he knew. Once he understood the full extent, he would search the catalogs for suitable items.

He would not have his wife looking like a waif! Or worst still, have people thinking he was too mean or thoughtless to buy his wife new clothes

"Edward." He came back to reality when she gently tugged at his arm.

Just the mere act of looking into her face softened him. The light perfume she wore drifted into his nostrils. It was *Le Secret d'une Fleur – Origan*, a fragrance he'd come to love. He secretly called it *Essence of Phoebe*.

He'd found the lone bottle on the shelf when he was checking the stocks. He'd presented it to her that evening. The delight on her face was almost more than he could bear.

I've never had perfume before, she'd declared, and it near broke his heart. Tears of joy welled in her eyes, and he'd watched as she'd fought them back.

In that moment he'd vowed to spoil his wife. To give her beautiful things. But he knew she would reject his gifts, and he'd have to fight her. She had a stubborn streak, that wife of his.

Little did she know he was in the process of placing an order for more dresses and women's necessities. But they would take some time to arrive.

"Edward," she said again, more loudly this time. "Are you alright? You seem… I don't know what. In a dream perhaps?"

He finally came out of his trance, snapping shut the order book for fear she would see what he was doing. "Sorry, I was miles away. Just thinking about… things. Work things," he quickly added.

She frowned. Had she read his mind? "Luncheon is ready. It's not like you to be late."

He smiled. "Thank you, Phoebe." He walked briskly to the door and turned over the sign, indicating the Mercantile was closed.

Together they went to the kitchen, his arm around her waist. This was a first. He'd never had the courage to put his arm around his wife like that before.

He washed his hands in the bathroom, then entered the kitchen.

"Sit." A mug of welcomed coffee was placed in front of him. He looked over the top of the mug at her. He wished she would wear her fiery red hair loose. She tied it up every day and doing so made her appear harsh.

She was far from that. Letting her hair hang loose softened her face.

As she placed the biscuits near him, he inhaled the enticing aroma. He stared at them. They looked different today.

He snatched one up and buttered it, then took a bite. He closed his eyes and savored the taste. Bliss. "Cheese biscuits," he said. "These are amazing, Phoebe."

She stared at him. "Really?" Her smile lit up her entire face.

"You are becoming a wonderful cook," he said. "You're a quick learner."

She clapped her hands together. "Mrs Mac used to tell me that," she said, then suddenly clamped her mouth shut.

"Mrs Mac?" he asked between mouthfuls.

"Forget it. She's not important now." He watched as the happiness left her face, and wondered who Mrs Mac was, and what she'd done to Phoebe. She'd obviously caused her great harm, and it saddened him.

"Sit and eat with me," he told her, eager for the smile to grace her face again. She did as he asked and sipped her tea before placing a cheese biscuit on her plate.

"Oooh, they are nice," she said, happy once more.

It didn't take much to make his Phoebe happy. He again wondered what tragedy had devastated her life.

* * *

"Phoebe," Edward had said a few days later, as she tidied up the kitchen after breakfast. "I think it's time you explored."

She stared at him. *What was he talking about?*

"Dayton Falls, I mean. You haven't really seen our little town, and it's time you did."

She continued to stare and shook her head. "Only if you come with me."

He stepped in closer to her. "I'm sorry, my love, but I can't. I have to take care of the store."

"I don't want to go out there alone," she said quietly. She was happy in her little domain here in their spacious flat. Wandering about making beds, cooking, sweeping, and cleaning up – it all made her happy.

Thinking back, she couldn't recall a time she'd been outside alone. Ever.

It was a scary thought, and she didn't want to do that.

"You'll be safe," Edward said confidently. Had he picked up on her lack of self-assurance?

She shook her head slowly.

"I'll stand outside and keep an eye on you. I promise."

She still wasn't convinced, but knew she had to try for his sake. "Alright then, I'll give it a try."

"Get some meat from the butcher. Perhaps for a roast? Mr Simpson will know what you need."

A roast? Was he losing his mind? She'd never cooked a roast and had no idea how to go about it.

Despite her misgivings, she nodded, and he continued. "Tell him to put it on my account."

The moment Edward left to start work, Phoebe prepared for her visit to the butcher. She had no decent coat, so prepared to brave the cold. Dayton Falls could be quite chilly at times, much colder than she was used to.

Sliding her thin jacket on her arms, she snatched up a basket and made her way to the store.

Edward had just finished serving a customer as she entered, so was able to put all his attention on her. His eyes bore into her, and she wasn't sure if she'd done something to cause his dismay, or whether it was the jacket.

He opened a notebook and scribbled something down but said not a word. He then opened the door to her. As she walked away, he issued instructions.

"Take a stroll down the street, and check out some of the other stores," he told her. "You might need them one day."

She looked back at him over her shoulder. What she really wanted to do was run back inside and hide behind her husband.

This was an adventure, but not one she savored. At least he would be watching to ensure she was safe. *But what if a customer arrived?* Then he'd be gone.

She swallowed. *It shouldn't be that hard.* Unfortunately, for her it was.

Phoebe straightened her back and stiffened her shoulders. She'd faced situations far greater than this one. She could not show fear. *Would not show fear.*

She glanced across the street until she saw the sign to the butcher's shop. Her heart was pounding, but she pushed forward. Crossing the road, she lifted her skirts to avoid getting them dirty.

Barely moving her head, she checked her husband was still there. He was. It gave her the fortitude to continue.

She would show him she had grit, even if she didn't feel quite as gutsy as she tried to make out.

She walked past the Barber Shop, as well as the Seamstress, glancing in the windows as she did. She glimpsed the sign to the Sheriff's Office, then rushed past until she reached her destination.

Did he have a *wanted* sign with her picture on it? She certainly hoped not.

As she opened the door to the butcher's shop, she was relieved to see a familiar face. "Good morning, Mrs Jensen," Phoebe said, her hands still shaking from her ordeal. "I have your name right, don't I?" She held her breath waiting for an answer.

"Good morning Phoebe. Yes, you do." The older woman smiled at her, glancing quickly at her bare head. Despite that, she seemed friendly enough.

Mr Simpson suddenly appeared from a backroom. He approached the counter with a package, which he handed to Mrs Jensen. "Put it on the account, Mrs Jensen?" he asked.

"Thank you, yes. Oh, Mr Simpson, this is Mrs Horvard. She's new in town."

After they'd exchanged pleasantries and Mrs Jensen left them, Phoebe told the butcher what her husband had requested.

He went out back again and returned with a package that looked similar to the one Mrs Jensen had left with.

"Mr Simpson," she said quietly despite the shop being devoid of other customers. "I have no idea what to do with this. Can you help me?" She felt two inches tall asking for such assistance, but what was she to do?

She grimaced as he fought back a smile, then slowly explained the steps to cooking a roast. Phoebe's relief was palpable.

"Thank you very much, Mr Simpson," she said as she opened the door.

"Anytime, Mrs Horvard," he said. "I am always happy to help."

She stood outside the shop, and looking back at the Mercantile, discovered Edward was still standing there. He gave her a wave, and she waved back. *What sort of wife was she to need her husband to stand guard to ensure her peace of mind?*

She walked in the opposite direction of the Mercantile, as Edward had instructed.

Next door was the Post Office. It might come in handy one day, but on second thoughts, perhaps not. She had no family, and no one to write too. Except her friends at the Burlesque. Was it worth the risk? Mr Grayson might find the letters and discover where she was and drag her back.

She let out a small shriek. No, she couldn't risk it.

With just the saddlery and livery at the end of the row, she crossed the street again, avoiding the blacksmith and newspaper office.

She continued along the sidewalk until she came to the Millinery, where she stared longingly in the window.

Phoebe gawked at the array of beautiful hats on display. She put a hand to her head – she didn't possess even a bonnet, let alone a hat as attractive as these.

Perhaps one day she would.

She sighed. That would never happen because she didn't have money. She'd never wished for beautiful things before, because she'd never had them. *You force yourself not to wish for those things that are totally out of reach.*

In the short time she'd been in Dayton Falls, Edward had spoiled her. He'd given her stunning dresses, perfume, and much more.

But the most important thing he'd given her was a home. A safe place to live.

And for that she would be eternally grateful.

She continued her travels, and to her surprise, the Mercantile was right next door.

Edward was nowhere in sight.

She watched through the window to find him serving a customer. She hadn't known he was missing, and she survived.

This time.

Would she risk it again? It had been quite an ordeal for her, not having done such a thing before.

Edward opened the door for his customer and greeted her. "Did you enjoy yourself?" he asked flippantly.

She stared up at him open-mouthed. He really had no idea how hard that had been for her. "Not really, but I did enjoy the Millinery."

He frowned. "You didn't enjoy getting out," he asked, quite taken aback.

She looked about, ensuring there were no prying ears. "Edward," she said, a little more forcefully than she'd intended. "I have *never* been outside alone before." Except for the night she ran away, she silently added. And that was terrifying.

They stared into each other's eyes for nearly a minute, then she lifted her skirts and pushed her way inside.

"But Phoebe," he called after her. "That can't be right."

She stopped at the entrance to the private residence and glared at him. "Are you sure?" she said quietly, then continued on her way.

When she looked back over her shoulder, she watched Edward shake his head. Perhaps he was learning more about her than he ever wanted to know.

Chapter Seven

Phoebe felt more nervous today than she had when she arrived.

She was attending church for the first time since their marriage. The preacher hadn't seemed too keen to meet her then, and she wondered what his reception to her would be like today.

Edward looked very smart in his Sunday best suit. She would straighten his tie, and they'd be on their way.

But he had other ideas.

"I have a surprise for you," he said.

She shook her head. He was always giving her surprises and gifts, and he shouldn't.

"Wait here." He almost ran to the bedroom and returned with a large package. "Open it."

He stood back grinning from ear to ear. Her curiosity was piqued.

She tore at the wrapping then stood back. It looked like a hat box. Could it be? Her heart skipped a beat.

Slowly she pulled off the lid and pulled out the bonnet. It was made of emerald green silk. Her heart sped up. How did he know she dreamed of a hat or bonnet?

She leaned into him and hugged him tight. "Oh Edward. This is beautiful. Thank you so much!"

"Go to the mirror and put in on," he said, unhooking himself from his wife.

She didn't need to be told twice. Phoebe ran to the bathroom and put the hat to her head. Edward had insisted she leave her hair down today, and now she knew why.

Pulling the bonnet on her head, she stared at her reflection. The color perfectly suited her red hair. *Did Edward see her staring at the hats in the Millinery?* No matter, she couldn't recall seeing this one in the window.

As she tied the emerald green bow, she noticed the detail on the bonnet. It had stunning ruffles near the front and was puffed out at the back. She would be able to wear it with her hair up as well.

Her heart fluttered. She didn't know if that was because of the bonnet itself, or because Edward cared enough to buy it for her.

Edward came up behind her and stared at her reflection. "It's beautiful," she said quietly. "Thank you."

"You look even more beautiful," he said, stroking her long hair. "I didn't think that was possible."

She blushed at his compliment. "The color is perfect."

He grinned. "I had it made especially for you." He leaned in and kissed her cheek, and Phoebe felt warmth go down her spine.

"You'll go to the Millinery tomorrow for fittings," Edward said. "I have ordered and paid for more, but you will choose this time." He smiled briefly, then turned away. "We must go," he said. "Or we'll be late for church, and that just won't do."

More? Edward had ordered more hats for her? When would she use them all?

He put a finger to her lips. "No argument. It's done."

Phoebe hooked her arm through his, and they went on their way. This was a much more comfortable way to be outside, she decided. With her husband by her side.

She discovered a few more stores on their way, including a dress shop and boot store. Edward caught her staring.

"They are beautiful boots for sure," he said, then lifted the bottom of her skirts slightly. "That's next on the agenda."

She was beginning to realize it was pointless to argue, so nodded her head briefly.

As they neared the tiny chapel, Phoebe heard music and began to sway to the beat. Edward stared at her. "I love music," she whispered as they neared the doorway.

"Mr and Mrs Horvard," the preacher said as he greeted them at the door. "Welcome."

They slid into a seat at the back and waited for the service to begin. Phoebe looked around the building, with its intricately carved ceilings and columns, and it's stained-glass windows.

"It's beautiful here," she whispered. How did she not notice all this the day they married? *Probably because she was exhausted and nervous.*

"It's no different to other churches," he whispered back.

Phoebe licked her lips. Should she tell him? "This is the first *real* church I've ever been in," she admitted quietly.

His expression was one of shock, but the service began, much to Phoebe's relief, meaning he didn't get to respond.

After the service, everyone stayed for coffee and cookies, as well as socializing. Many of the parishioners lived well out of town, Edward told her. This was often their only chance to see other town folk.

He introduced her to the regulars, as he'd called them. Perhaps she would start to make some friends? She hoped so.

She left an hour later with a cacophony of names and faces in her head. Her one fear was getting people's names confused.

"You did well," he said as they strolled back home.

Home. She did now think of it as home. It was the only real home she could remember having.

Edward tightened his grip on her waist.

It was time. She needed to tell him of her past. Snippets of her life were making their way from her memories and out of her mouth.

She didn't want him to find out she was a wanted woman from the sheriff.

"I," Where did she start? "I have to tell you something," she said.

He stared at her but didn't interrupt.

"The reason I had to come here in a hurry."

He quickly shushed her. "Not here. Prying ears and all." He pulled her closer. "Besides, I don't want you to feel compelled to tell me anything."

Her lips pulled into a tight line. He'd given her so much, and she'd given him so little in return. She owed him this much, and she would see to it her heard her out.

She just didn't know when that would be.

* * *

Edward sat down to his first roast supper since his marriage just a few weeks ago. Was it really only such a short time?

He stared down at his plate. Roast pork, apple sauce, and vegetables. Phoebe had really outdone herself this time.

He wiped his mouth with a clean napkin, then took a sip of coffee. His belly was full, and his heart was too.

What he really wanted to do was infiltrate the walls that Phoebe had put up between them. His life was an open book, but she was living in the shadows.

Every now and then she let something slip, like her comment about *Mrs Mac*, then she suddenly pulled down the shutters.

Trying to get her to open up had so far proved impossible.

She leaned into him and took his dirty dishes, and he began to stand.

"Where are you going," she asked with a sly smile. "I have a surprise for you." She touched his shoulder and guided him back into his chair.

He relished her touch – it was not something she did often. In fact, they rarely made physical contact, but when they did, sparks flew. At least for him they did. He had no idea about Phoebe.

She lifted an item from the counter top and placed it on the table. It was covered with a kitchen towel, so she really had meant it to be a surprise.

He reached over to remove the kitchen towel, his curiosity getting the better of him. She slapped his hand away.

The contact was brief, but he relished it. As she pulled away, he reached for her hand again.

"Phoebe," he said softly. "I like it when you touch me."

She froze for just a moment, then giggled and proceeded to prepare for his surprise. "Are you ready?" She sounded as excited as a teenager.

It made his heart sing. When she was happy and excited, it lifted his mood.

"Close your eyes."

He did as he was told. "Now open them."

She had the kitchen towel in her hand and was pointing. "Is it pie?" he asked excitedly. He hadn't had pie for a very long time. It felt like forever.

"Apple pie," she said. "And cream!"

"Oh my Lord," he said. "You are quite the cook now, Phoebe," he said, grabbing for her hand, and kissing it softly.

He stared up into her face. She looked shocked. Was that because he kissed her hand, or did she feel the things he was feeling?

Did her heart do a little flutter when he touched her? And did the butterflies in her stomach all come to life when they connected?

She snatched her hand back out of his light grip. "I, I need to get a knife and cut this up," she said, pulling away.

She reached into the cupboard and pulled out two bowls, then served them each a piece of pie.

"I'm a rich man," he said.

She glared at him.

He stumbled to explain himself. "I don't mean rich with money, although I am that too," he said. "I'm rich in another way. I won the lottery when they sent you to me." He might not have thought that at first, but now he knew better.

Her glare turned into a sweet smile. He reached for her hand again and indicated for her to sit down. "I admit to having misgivings when you arrived," he said, looking at the table. "But you have proven yourself time and again."

His voice suddenly dropped. "I'm falling in love with you, Phoebe," he said quietly. "I didn't think I was capable of love, but you proved me wrong."

Her eyes never left his. "I don't know if I'm in love or not," she said. "Since I've never been in love as far as I know."

He chuckled, but she ignored him and continued.

"When you are close, I feel a little flutter in my belly."

He stood and pulled her up with him, enveloping her in a big hug. "Oh Phoebe," he said into her ear. "That happens to me too."

They stood there for what seemed a lifetime.

"I don't know about you," she said forcefully, but I want some of that pie I slaved over for hours."

The pie was tempting, there was no doubt, but given the choice, he'd hold his wife in his arms until eternity.

* * *

Phoebe vowed that tonight she would tell her husband everything.

She would not fall asleep before he arrived like she usually did. She swore to stay awake and confess to all her sins.

Not that they were her fault, because she was a victim of circumstances, but that didn't make it any better.

She went to the bathroom for her ablutions, her heart racing at the thought of what she was about to do. As she brushed her hair, she knew she was stalling for time.

Standing in her beautiful nightgown, staring at her reflection, she wondered what his reaction would be.

Would he send her away once he found out?

 "Edward," she said quietly, finding him already in the bedroom. "I want to you know, you've done far more for me in these short weeks, than anyone has done in my entire life."

He pulled her into a big bear hug. "Then they're fools," he said against her hair.

She rested her head against his chest. She'd hit the jackpot with this man. With Edward. She'd been right about him, he was kind. He cared about her, even though she was still a virtual stranger.

She hoped that would change someday soon.

She looked down at the bed he had turned back, ready for them.

She remembered back to the first time she'd slept with Edward. She'd been terrified as it would be her first time sharing her bed with a man. In some ways, tonight was worse.

Tonight, she would reveal her sordid life story.

As she climbed into bed, Edward sat on the opposite side, removing his shoes and socks. When he began to unbutton his shirt, she turned away. She'd never seen a man undress in her life and wasn't about to start now.

She heard the wardrobe door open then close and felt his weight on the bed. He turned off the light and shuffled across toward her.

His arm came around her, resting on her belly. She stiffened.

"Do you mind?" he asked gently. "I'd like to hold my beautiful wife, if that's alright?"

Had he predicted she was preparing to bare her soul? To put herself out there to him?

"I don't mind," she finally said, relaxing. If she was truthful, she liked the feel of him against her. And she certainly enjoyed being held by him.

It was a nice feeling and made her feel warm and fuzzy inside, even though she knew she shouldn't.

She found herself shuffling even closer toward him. The closer the better. "This is nice," she said softly. "And the bed is very comfortable. I've only ever slept on hard mattresses until I came here."

His grip tightened on her and he pulled her a little closer. "Phoebe," he said softly. "I know your arrival here was urgent, and we've skirted around it a lot, but would you mind telling me the circumstances?"

She stiffened again.

"I'll understand if you don't want to."

His words were quiet and comforting.

She hesitated at first, but then let it all spill out. By the time she finished, tears were rolling down her cheeks. She hadn't realized how terrified she'd been until this moment.

He didn't say a word, just held her tightly. *Had she repulsed him that much?*

Finally, he broke the silence. "I'm so sorry you had to endure that, Phoebe," he said next to her ear. "I want you to think of our marriage as a new start to your life."

She nodded – she would happily do that if she could.

"It's been a new start for me as well," he said. "I wasn't living before. You've brought sunshine into my life. Into my heart."

Phoebe fell asleep in the arms of her husband. She realized later, she wouldn't want it any other way.

Chapter Eight

"There's a dance Saturday night," Edward announced. "It will be the highlight of the month."

Phoebe's eyes sparkled and heat colored her cheeks. "Oh yes please!"

He watched her pace the floor. "But what should I wear? I don't know about such things," she said, a scowl on her face.

"Phoebe," he said, strolling over to her and taking her by the shoulders. "It's not a big deal. Honestly."

"It's a big deal to me," she said, pouting. "I wouldn't know what to wear though." She sighed as he let go of her.

"You can wear your Sunday best if that's what you want, my love."

He had felt even closer to Phoebe since she'd disclosed her past life, and he loved her even more for the trust she'd placed in him.

Despite all that, they still hadn't consummated their marriage.

He couldn't wait for the day they had youngsters running around, although there would have to be ground rules. They couldn't have children running in and out of the Mercantile, torturing customers with their antics.

He couldn't help but smile at the thought.

"What are you smiling about?" Her words brought Edward out of his revelry.

"Nothing really. Oh, we have to provide a plate of food," he said. "For the dance. Everyone contributes something."

A slow smile crossed her face. "At least I can cook now," she said, tapping her chin. "What should I take?"

The store was void of customers, and Phoebe had been helping out. Even with her store apron on, she looked stunning. What had he done to deserve such a beauty?

"Cheese biscuits perhaps," he offered. "Or maybe some muffins. Those you made the other day were delicious."

She blushed at his compliment.

"I've been thinking," Edward said, completely changing the subject. "How would you feel about supplying the store with your delicious baked goods?"

Phoebe frowned, then thought for a minute. "What would that entail?"

He rubbed a hand across his chin. Why his previous supplier, the sheriff's sister, had to move away and open her own bakery, he'd never understand.

"Muffins, oatmeal cookies, pound cake. That sort of thing. And not every day."

She frowned again. "If I could rotate through them, and not have to make them all every day, then perhaps."

He nodded. "That sounds quite practical," he said.

"I won't let you down, Edward. I appreciate your trust in me." Phoebe almost knocked him over in her haste to hug him. For the first time ever, her lips covered his. It was a chaste kiss, and one meant to be in thanks, he was sure. He saw it as a first step toward making their relationship more intimate.

He stared down at her for a few moments, then his arms went gently up around her, and he deepened the kiss. Not too much though, but enough to let her know he liked it, and also to convey it was quite acceptable. Her eyes were closed, and her face relaxed. She even looked like she was enjoying it.

The tinkle of the bell had her stepping away from him in record time.

The timing had him cursing under his breath. "Good afternoon Mrs Grogan," he said, as he reluctantly stepped away from his wife and toward his ill-timed customer.

* * *

Phoebe's heart pounded.

She was so excited about going to the dance tonight. "My cider cake should be cooled now," she told her husband.

"You go and get ready. I'll be closing the store soon."

Phoebe finished preparing supper. They didn't need much because there would be a heap of food at the dance, Edward had told her.

She couldn't wait.

She pulled out one of their best plates and proceeded to cut the cider cake into pieces. She carefully laid it on the plate, then set it aside.

The soup was almost ready, and the hot cakes were cooling. She set the table, then went to the bedroom to set out her clothes.

Edward had surprised her with a big box of clothes. Dresses of all sorts, casual and formal. Shawls and coats, and plenty of undergarments.

He was beyond kind.

She chose one if the dresses for the dance, her favorite out of all the dresses he'd bought for her. The dress had tiny blue roses printed on the material cream colored soft material. It had a high neckline made of lace, and buttons down the torso, complimenting the layered material. The sleeves were long, puffed at the shoulder, and buttoned above the wrist, with matching lace cascading over her wrist.

It was the most beautiful dress she'd ever owned. He'd also bought her a matching pale blue shawl.

Edward really did spoil her and she could imagine how other women would be envious of her.

She had just finished placing her flowered hat on her head when Edward said it was time to leave.

Phoebe scooped up the plate of cider cake, which she had covered with a pretty kitchen towel, and prepared herself for the unknown.

These last weeks had been a journey of unknowns, most of them delightful to the new bride.

She made her way downstairs, and Edward hooked his arm through hers.

It was a little chilly outside, and she pulled the shawl up around her shoulders. "You'll have fun," Edward said gently. "You'll see."

"I'm not worried," she replied, then stared into his eyes. "Alright, maybe just a little. I won't know most of those people."

He patted her hand. "You soon will." He smiled at her and they continued the short trek to the church hall.

She heard faint music as they approached, and her heart did a flutter. Of course, she knew there would be music, it was a dance, but she tried not to get her hopes up.

When they arrived, there were a few familiar faces. Mrs Jensen was there, along with Mrs Green and Mrs Jackson. Their husbands were also in attendance. The men were congregated in one corner, with the women in the other.

Music played in the background.

Mrs Jensen approached them. "Phoebe, it's so nice to see you, my dear. We don't get to see a lot of you."

Phoebe still held onto her offering for the night. "Let me take that, my dear. In fact, you come with me and I'll introduce you to some of the other women."

She looked to Edward for reassurance and he nodded. "I'll be right here," he told her.

As she walked away, Phoebe glanced back over her shoulder, but realized she was being childish. Her husband would still be there when she got back. He told her he would, and she trusted him.

In the kitchen she was introduced to more people than she'd ever remember, then they returned to the main hall.

The musicians tuned their instruments for the last time, and one shouted above the din. "Prepare to dance!"

A circle was formed, and Edward invited her onto the floor. Phoebe was quite dismayed to learn she would be shuffled about the room, a new partner for each round. She did eventually land back with her husband, but then the music stopped.

What a disappointment.

Everyone had taken a seat when soft music began.

A young man bolted up and asked her to dance. "You look so pretty," he told her, a glint in his eye.

"I, I…" She didn't know what to do or to say.

Edward stepped behind him. "Are you asking my wife to dance, sonny?" he asked, his annoyance evident. The potential suitor scurried off, leaving Edward grinning after him.

"May I have this dance?" he asked, a grin still on his face.

Phoebe looked around. Only a few couples were on the dance floor, and she didn't want to make a spectacle of herself, but Edward insisted.

He pulled her to her feet, and his arms went around her. Slowly, one by one, more couples joined them, making Phoebe a little more comfortable.

She gazed into his eyes. Edward looked relaxed and very happy. He seldom presented that way in public. She rested her head against his chest and relaxed into him.

They gently rocked to the rhythm of the music, moving as one. Phoebe felt more connected to Edward than she had ever been.

He suddenly leaned down and kissed her cheek, and she felt the heat creep up her face. "Edward!" she whispered.

His voice was soft in her ear. "I'm allowed," he said quietly. "We're married, remember?" He chuckled and straightened up.

She felt several eyes on them.

The music suddenly stopped, and everyone clapped. As they were about to return to their seats, the music started up again. This time it was even slower than before.

"Stay with me, Phoebe?"

She was enjoying herself. It might not be the sort of dancing she was used to, but she loved any kind of dancing.

She nodded as she looked into his sparkling blue eyes. This time he led her outside the hall, despite her protests.

"It's less crowded out here," he said. "But we can still hear the music."

He put his arms around her again, only this time more intimately. One hand sat on her waist, as the other came up her back. She leaned into him, and he pulled her even closer.

The music was calming, and they gently rocked to the beat together. Edward let go one of his hands and used it to lift her chin, until they were staring into each other's eyes.

The moonlight played across his face, softening his features. "Phoebe," he said softly. "I am so in love with you."

He stared at her and waited for her reaction. She licked her lips and gazed at his mouth.

His head came down and his lips covered hers. A tingle went down her spine and her heart fluttered.

One hand went up her back, and the other caressed her cheek. She heard herself groan.

He suddenly pulled back and looked about, for witnesses to his indiscretion no doubt, and she felt bereft.

"Edward," she whispered. "I love you too. I have almost from the day we met."

He lifted her in his arms like she was a child and swung her about.

"Edward, you put me down this instance," she said emphatically.

He put her down but stood grinning at her.

"What?" she asked, hands on her hips.

"You're such a tiny thing, but I love it when you're forceful," he said, right before he swooped in and kissed her again.

They walked home in silence after the dance was over.

"I had a wonderful time," Phoebe said gazing into her husband's moonlit face.

"I did too."

She'd enjoyed the music and danced most of the night away. She only stopped to help the ladies in the kitchen, which didn't take very long. The clean up afterwards was more time consuming though.

They were totally alone on the street. Most people had arrived by wagon; they were lucky to live so close.

"Edward," she said softly. "We've been married for a while now…"

"Nearly three months."

"And we haven't… you know…" She felt herself blush, thankful for the darkness surrounding them.

"Consummated our marriage?" he said with a chuckle.

"Uh, yes," she whispered, feeling somewhat embarrassed.

He patted her hand.

"I think it's time," she said, feeling rather starry-eyed and dreamy after the time they'd spent together. She'd seen a whole new side of Edward tonight, and it certainly didn't upset her.

The stuffy Mercantile owner was gone, and the romantic husband had stepped in. Not that he wasn't romantic at home, because he was. He plowed her with gifts on a constant basis and praised her every chance he got.

When they arrived at the Mercantile, she turned to face him. "Edward," she said quietly. "I've never had any contact with children. Except at the orphanage."

There, she'd said it.

He stared into her blue eyes, then leaned in and kissed her. His arms wrapped around her, then he reached down and lifted her gently.

"What are you doing?" she whispered.

"Taking you to bed."

As much as she was apprehensive, she was ecstatic to finally become a real wife to her wonderful husband.

Chapter Nine

A few weeks later, Sheriff Angus Doyle strolled into the Mercantile, determination written all over his face.

"Phoebe," he said quietly. "Could I have a word?"

She stared at him, her heart racing. *Had the law finally caught up with her?* She straightened up from the task at hand, stacking the shelves with new supplies, her hands visibly shaking, sick dread washing over her. She should have known her happiness couldn't last.

Edward strolled over and stood steadfastly by her side. "What is it, Sheriff?" he asked, his voice gruff.

Sheriff Doyle looked around. There were customers in the store, and Phoebe wondered if he would embarrass her in front of them.

His voice dropped to barely above a whisper. "Come to the Sheriff's office. The sooner the better."

She nodded and finished up her task.

Her legs felt weak, and she felt sure she would faint, but she wasn't going to show weakness in front of her husband. She wouldn't allow herself to faint. Nor would she become hysterical.

It was time. The sheriff had discovered she was a wanted woman, and was about to deal with her. She'd be locked in jail within the hour.

Stony faced, Edward stood close to her, giving her much needed support. "Don't worry," he said quietly. "We'll sort it out."

Tears stung the back of her eyes, but she refused to allow them freedom.

They hugged each other – they knew this day may come.

Edward dealt with the remaining customers, then put up the *closed* sign.

"Ready?" Edward was white as a sheet, and she was certain she would be too.

She nodded and started for the door despite her lightheadedness. Edward pulled her close and gave her the support she needed.

He locked the door to the Mercantile, then they slowly crossed the road to the Sheriff's Office, her mind racing.

She should have given herself up in the beginning; the punishment might not have been so bad. And what of Edward's reputation in the town? Married to a wanted woman, a criminal.

Phoebe stood outside momentarily, taking in deep breaths, preparing herself for the worst.

Her loving husband opened the door, then guided her gently inside.

"Sit down," Sheriff Doyle said, indicating the chairs in front of his well-worn desk.

Phoebe put her hands out in front of her ready to be handcuffed.

The sheriff laughed, and she took offence at his insolence.

"I'm ready to go to jail," she said in a quiet voice. "But I'd like to pack a bag first."

He looked sternly at Edward. "You don't need to be here, but I can understand you wanting to."

She looked up at her husband who straightened his shoulders. "I am not going anywhere Sheriff."

"Please yourself."

He turned to Phoebe. "I've made some enquiries about your situation," he said, glancing at each of them. "Got the Westlake Sheriff to check out your story."

Phoebe swallowed and forced back a sob.

"What you told Edward about the Burlesque was true," he said. "They were using it to force young women to become prostitutes. Soiled doves."

"You told him?" she accused her husband, but he only tightened his grip on her.

Sheriff Doyle leaned toward her and she cringed. "Because of you, both the Burlesque and the Gentleman's Club have been closed down. Mr Grayson is in jail."

Her lips quivered. *Could it really be true?*

"What is going to happen to me," she asked quietly, her voice breaking.

The sheriff leaned back in his seat. "To you? You did nothing wrong and are free to go." He smiled, but Phoebe wasn't sure there was anything to smile about.

"What about the contract I had with Mr Grayson?" Her eyes strayed from the sheriff to her husband.

Edward squeezed her shoulder tight.

Sheriff Doyle shoved his chair back and stood. "It's invalid. It was never legal. He's broken so many laws he'll be in jail for a very long time."

"Phoebe," he said, coming to stand beside her. "You have no idea how many young women you've saved. Because of you, we were able to rescue dozens of young women who had been forced into prostitution. Running away was a courageous thing to do. You should be congratulated for doing it."

Edward pulled her into his arms and held her tight. Her relief was so palpable tears rolled down her cheeks. Her legs went so weak, she could barely hold herself up, and before she knew it, Edward had lifted her and started back to the Mercantile.

He turned back as he stepped out of the Sheriff's Office, his hand outstretched. "Thank you, Sheriff," he said, his voice breaking. "I don't know how we can ever repay you."

"Knowing Phoebe is safe here in Dayton Falls is the only thanks I need."

Edward nodded and carried his beautiful wife home.

* * *

Phoebe finished the last of her baking and left it to cool.

Edward was busy in the store – she could hear him talking to customers. The little bell was tinkling constantly.

He'd been right, offering baked goods again had been a boon to the store.

She entered the store, her hands full with this morning's baking efforts, to see a group of town's people staring at her. There were even a few men.

It startled her.

"What's on offer today, Mrs Horvard," Mr Carson asked. "I want to surprise my wife."

She smiled. "What a lovely gesture, Mr Carson," she said, and genuinely meant it. "I have apple muffins, and pound cake in this batch. Upstairs cooling are cookies and carrot cake."

He stretched his neck to see. "I'll take six apple muffins," he said. "Before someone else beats me to it."

Edward took the plate from Phoebe and placed six muffins in a brown paper bag, then pulled her close to his side. "She's a great cook, my wife," he said proudly.

Phoebe felt the heat creep up her face, but was pleased to be so well thought of, not only by her husband who doted on her, but also by others.

"I'll take the other six," Mrs Carlisle said quickly. "I hate baking," she whispered to Phoebe.

The bell over the door tinkled and all the customers turned to see who was joining them. "Good morning, Mrs Jones," Edward said, looking the very pregnant woman over. "Should you be out and about in your condition?"

She lived right across the road behind the Barber's Shop, but still, it would have been an effort.

Phoebe snatched up a chair for her to sit on. "Does Mr Jones know you're here," she asked, concerned for her friend.

"I'm sure he saw me totter over," she said, almost smiling. "I have a list of supplies I need before our baby arrives." She patted her belly. "And Phoebe, can I get some of your baked goods? Charlie loves cakes and muffins."

Finally, after all these years of living, Phoebe felt she had found her calling and found the love of her life.

Epilogue

Ten months later…

"Seriously Phoebe," Edward said assertively. "You need to stop."

She glared at him.

"*Please*," he begged. "Sit down. Have a rest. I can finish stacking these shelves."

"Just because I am with child, doesn't mean I'm an invalid." She pouted at him as she did every time she didn't get her own way.

He threw his arms up in the air. "Fine." Instead of arguing further, he leaned down and picked up the remainder of the stock she was packing.

"Hey! I need those." She stood with her hands on her hips.

He frowned. His wife would be the death of him – she was too independent for her own good.

She pushed the chair away. "Honestly, you're fussing for nothing."

She turned to walk away from him. "Oh, oh, no!"

Phoebe floundered and he reached for her. "What is it?" he asked, his face aching from worry.

She didn't say a word but pointed to the floor.

Panic rose up his chest, and his heart pounded. He started pacing the floor trying to think. "Waters broke," he muttered under his breath. "What should I do?" He continued to pace.

"Edward," she said assertively. "Go and get Doc Grogan. I'll go and lay down."

He started out the door then quickly turned back. "Oh no you don't. You can't do that alone." He took her arm and gently helped her into the residence, and onto the bed. "You stay there, and don't move!"

He gazed down at her laying on the bed, knowing he would soon be a father. "Phoebe," he said. "I love you more than life itself." He kneeled on the bed next to her and kissed her. "I'll be back shortly.

It seemed to take an eternity to reach the doctor's office, and he was panting when he got there. "Doc," he said between pants. "Phoebe's waters broke."

Doc Grogan grabbed his bag and headed to the Mercantile. "You round up Mrs Jensen. I'm going to need her help."

Edward did as he was told, then returned to the Mercantile where he was exiled for the duration of the birth, much to his disgust.

He sat outside the Mercantile, listening to Phoebe's screams, until he could take no more. He took himself over to the Barber's Shop.

"Haircut," Charlie Jones asked. "Or a refuge from the screams?"

"Both," Edward said, closing the door behind him, praying his amazing wife survived her ordeal.

* * *

Edward held his baby son close to his chest.

"Joshua Brennan Horvard," he said quietly. "You have an amazing mama."

He'd always been such a strong man. A man who would fight to the death for his wife if necessary. But today he'd been brought to tears both at the pain his darling Phoebe had endured, and at meeting his beautiful son.

He leaned in and kissed Joshua's forehead gently and the baby began to cry. "Here, you take him," he said, shoving Joshua back toward Phoebe.

Exhausted, she still managed to grin. "He's probably hungry," she said gently, attaching the baby to her breast for a feed.

The crying stopped immediately.

"Phoebe," Edward said, his voice breaking. "Thank you for this amazing gift of a son." He wiped a tear from his eyes. "And for coming into my life. I can't imagine life without you."

"I love you too," she said quietly as she drifted off to sleep.

He sat quietly on the side of the bed and watched the baby feed as his mother slept. He hoped there would be many more babies to come.

From the Author

Thank you so much for reading my book – I hope you enjoyed it.

I would greatly appreciate you leaving a review where you purchased, even if it is only a one-liner. It helps to have my books more visible!

~*~

The next book in this series is *The Blacksmith's Reluctant Bride*

From the Author

Thank you so much for reading my book – I hope you enjoyed it.

I would greatly appreciate you leaving a review where you purchased, even if it is only a one-liner. It helps to have my books more visible!

~*~

About the Author

Multi-published, award-winning and bestselling author Cheryl Wright, former secretary, debt collector, account manager, writing coach, and shopping tour hostess, loves reading.

She writes both historical and contemporary western romance, as well as romantic suspense.

She lives in Melbourne, Australia, and is married with two adult children and has six grandchildren. When she's not writing, she can be found in her craft room making greeting cards.

Links

Website: *http://www.cheryl-wright.com/*

Facebook   Reader   Group: *https://www.facebook.com/groups/cherylwrightaut hor/*

Join My Newsletter:

https://cheryl-wright.com/newsletter/
(and receive a free book)